4   5 billion years ago, our planet, Earth, forms.

3   1 billion years after the Big Bang, the galaxies begin to take shape.

8   2.5 billion years ago, our breathable atmosphere forms.

7   3 billion years ago, life begins with the appearance of the first bacteria and blue algae.

Tyrannosaurus

Argentinosaurus

Baryonyx

Vol. 6

Vol. 5

Vol. 4

Triceratops

Camarasaurus

Giganotosaurus

Scipionyx

Cretaceous

CONTENTS

First published in the United States of America in 2009 by Abbeville Press, 137 Varick Street, New York, NY 10013

First published in Italy in 2009 by Editoriale Jaca Book S.p.A., via Frua 11, 20146 Milano

First edition
10 9 8 7 6 5 4 3 2 1

Library of Congress Cataloging-in-Publication Data

Bacchin, Matteo.
    [Piccolo. English]
Dinosaurs growing up in the Cretaceous : Scipionyx / drawings and story, Matteo Bacchin ; essays and story, Marco Signore ; translated from the Italian by Marguerite Shore. -- 1st ed.
    p. cm. -- (Dinosaurs)
    ISBN 978-0-7892-1012-8 (alk. paper)
    1. Scipionyx--Juvenile literature. 2. Paleontology--Cretaceous--Juvenile literature. I. Signore, Marco. II. Title. III. Title: Scipionyx.
    QE862.S3B33413 2010
    567.9--dc22
                2009016831

For bulk and premium sales and for text adoption procedures, write to Customer Service Manager, Abbeville Press, 137 Varick Street, New York, NY 10013, or call 1-800-ARTBOOK.

Visit Abbeville Press online at www.abbeville.com.

For the English-language edition: Austin Allen, editor; Ashley Benning, copy editor; Louise Kurtz, production manager; Robert Weisberg, composition; Ada Blazer, cover design.

Foreword
By Mark Norell

Looking at the panoply of bizarre dinosaur anatomical structures, it is easy to conjure up images of medieval battle armor. Dinosaurs display everything from head and tail spikes, shield-like frills, and battering-ram heads to mace-like tail clubs and chain-mail neck armor. Yet as with everything else in paleontology, things get complicated if these structures are examined more closely. It turns out that many of them would perform poorly if they were used defensively, let alone offensively.

The head shields of ceratopsians, or horned dinosaurs, are a good example. The best known of these animals is *Triceratops*, and yes, it has a large, thick, solid shield. However, the shields of many of its close relatives are perforate—that is, formed only of an outline of very thin bone around large, window-like holes in the skull. Although they would have been covered with skin in life, they would have been quite delicate (in some of the smaller forms they are paper thin) and thus made very poor shields.

Similarly, how to understand the horns of these animals? They must have been impressive structures in life, as they were covered with keratin (the material found in claws and our fingernails), making them almost twice as large as the fossilized bones. But if they were often used in intraspecies battles or for defense, we would expect to see many damaged horns, whereas in fact we see remarkably few.

So what were these structures for? If we look at animals that have similar adaptations today, the horns and frills are used much more for display than for defense. Horned ungulates like deer and antelopes are a good example. In white-tailed deer the horns of males are much larger than those of females; you would think the females would need more protection, but it seems that the large male horns are aesthetically pleasing to females and used mainly to attract mates, not repel predators. Compare African antelopes, a species in which males and females have horns of nearly equal size. Here the horns are used as a signal to identify members of the same species, often in large interspecies herds. It is likely that many of the extreme body types seen in fossil animals had more to do with looking right than beating up on predators or enemies.

DINOSAURS

GROWING UP IN THE

CRETACEOUS

SCIPIONYX

DINOSAURS

Growing Up in the Cretaceous

SCIPIONYX

Drawings and story
MATTEO BACCHIN

Essays and story
MARCO SIGNORE

Translated from the Italian
by Marguerite Shore

ABBEVILLE KIDS
A Division of Abbeville Publishing Group
New York   London

IN THIS STORY

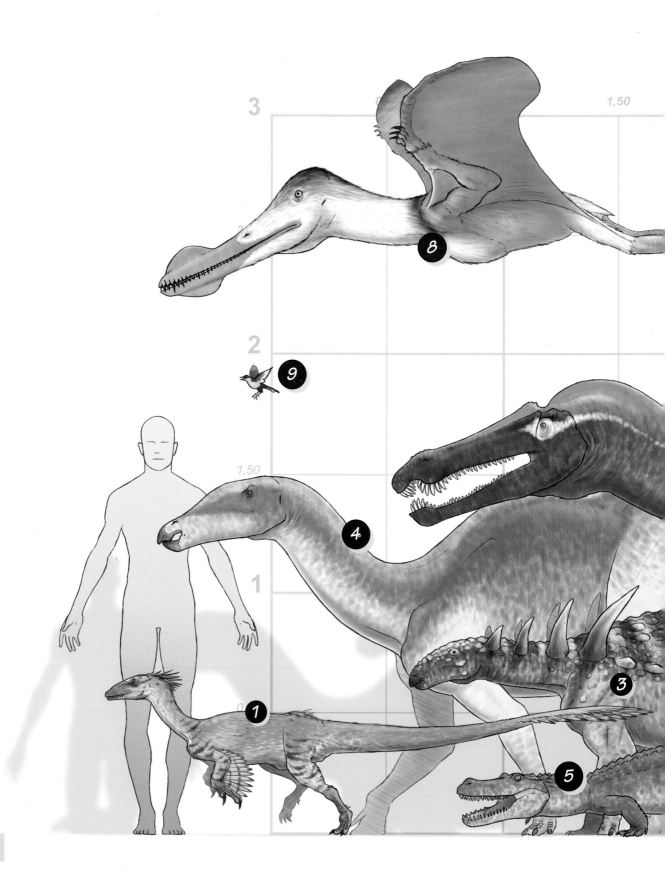

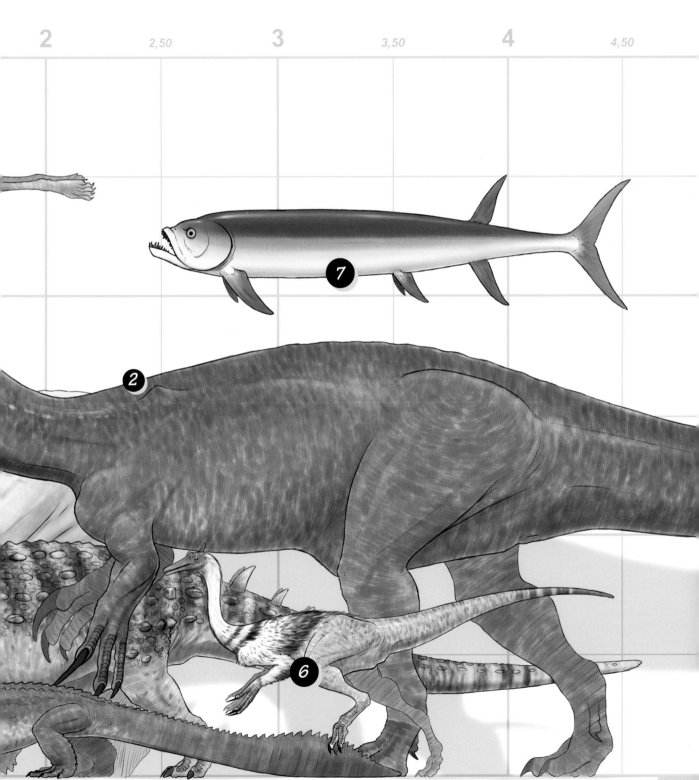

1 Scipionyx
2 Baryonyx
3 Nodosauridae
4 Iguanodontidae
5 Crocodile
6 Pelecanimimus
7 Ichthyodectidae
8 Ornithocheiridae
9 Iberomesornis

See identikit on page 40

2   2,50   3   3,50   4   4,50

THE NARRATOR

AS YOU KNOW, I AM A SUN. A YELLOW SUN.

NOT THE GREATEST, NOR EVEN THE ELDEST, OF MY BROTHER AND SISTER STARS, ALL BORN FROM THE ETERNAL SPARK OF THE COSMOS. THOUGH I AM YOUNG, I HAVE SEEN MANY THINGS—MUCH MORE THAN MANY OF THE OTHER SUNS SCATTERED THROUGH SPACE.

I AM FORTUNATE: MY ORBIT, IN THIS ARM OF THE GALAXY, IS NOT SOLITARY. VARIOUS WORLDS HAVE FORMED AROUND ME,

AND I HAVE WITNESSED AND OBSERVED MANY LIVES IN THE TIME I HAVE BEEN GRANTED SO FAR.

IN FACT, I WILL TELL YOU NOW ABOUT ONE EXTRAORDINARY LIFE FROM AN ASTONISHING PERIOD THAT EARTH, THE THIRD PLANET AND A JEWEL AMONG ALL OTHERS, WAS ABLE TO BRING TO FLOWER FROM THE ASHES OF A GREAT CATASTROPHE.

YOU HUMANS HAVE BEEN ABLE TO DISCOVER LOST ECHOES OF THIS TIME:

IN ROCK AMID ROCKS, STONE EVIDENCE BEARING THE MEMORY OF
THAT PAST ERA AND THE RACE OF CREATURES THAT LIVED THEN.

THE EONS HAVE EMPTIED THEIR CHESTS OF BREATH AND WARMTH
AND TRANSFORMED THEM INTO SILENT STONES. THEIR EMPTY
EYE SOCKETS STILL SEEM TO BE PIERCING YOU AS YOU ADMIRE THEM
IN MUSEUMS, HYPNOTIZING YOU WHILE YOU TRY TO INVESTIGATE THE
TWISTS AND TURNS OF THAT PRIMORDIAL TIME.

A DISTANT TIME—BEFORE THE PYRAMIDS, BEFORE THE GODS,
BEFORE THE ERA OF HUMAN BEINGS. BEFORE EVEN THE
MOST ANCIENT MEMORY OF THE WHALES. A TIME
WHEN THESE CREATURES, TAKING THE WIDEST
VARIETY OF FORMS, WERE THE UNCONTESTED
RULERS OF THE PLANET.

THEY CONQUERED EVERY CORNER OF THE EARTH,
WALKING THE GROUND LIKE NO PREVIOUS GENERATION;

AND THEY SUCCEEDED IN VENTURING INTO THE SKIES, AS NO
CREATURE HAD EVER DONE BEFORE, WITH THE HELP OF ONLY
DELICATE FEATHERS. THEY SEEMED INVINCIBLE—YET THEY
VANISHED UNDER MYSTERIOUS CIRCUMSTANCES, STILL TO
BE UNCOVERED.

AND SO, WHAT WILL MY NEXT STORY UNFOLD?

I HAVE TOLD YOU ABOUT THE LONG JOURNEY IN THE TIME
OF THE NEW TRACKS. I HAVE TOLD YOU ABOUT THE ERA OF
ASCENT, AND HOW AN ANCIENT FLYER BECAME A FOSSIL
AND A LEGEND, AND HOW THE LEADER OF THE PACK OF
THREE-CLAWED HUNTERS LOST HIS PLACE TO A YOUNG AND
SPIRITED RIVAL.

THIS TIME I WILL TELL YOU ABOUT THE AGE OF THE LAST
DINOSAURS—THE STORY OF AN EGG, AN INFANT, AND
AN ADULT. A STORY OF BIRTH AND DEATH.
A STORY OF LIFE.

I WILL TELL YOU ABOUT...

THE DINOSAURS

4 GROWING UP IN THE CRETACEOUS

THOUSANDS AND THOUSANDS OF SEASONS HAVE PASSED BETWEEN THE TIME WHEN THE PACK LEADER LOST HIS THRONE AND THE END OF THE ERA OF ASCENT. MULTIPLY THAT CYCLE THOUSANDS AND THOUSANDS OF TIMES OVER—THAT IS HOW MUCH TIME HAS PASSED BETWEEN THE ERA OF ASCENT AND WHAT I AM ABOUT TO DESCRIBE.

DURING THAT TIME THOUSANDS OF MOUNTAINS ROSE AND THEN TURNED TO DUST, MAKING WAY FOR THOUSANDS OF NEW MOUNTAINS. THOUSANDS OF OLD RIVERS RAN DRY AND THOUSANDS OF NEW ONES CARVED THEIR WAY SEAWARD, THOUSANDS OF TIMES. AND LIKE THE RIVERS, WE RETURN TO THAT PRIMORDIAL BUT EVER-YOUNG SEA FOR OUR STORY. IN THIS SULTRY ERA, IT HAS FLOODED VAST REGIONS OF THE EARTH, REACHING ITS GREATEST EXPANSE EVER.

THE LAGOONS AND ATOLLS HERE MAKE UP WHAT YOU WILL CALL ITALY. AS IN THE TIME OF THE ANCIENT WINGED CREATURES, THE LAGOON BELOW US IS ALSO THE HOME OF DROWSY CROCODILES THAT BASK IN MY NOONDAY LIGHT, AND WINGED LIZARDS THAT ROAM THE SKIES IN CONSTANT SEARCH OF FOOD.

BUT THEIR FACES ARE NEW IN THE ERA OF THE LAST DINOSAURS.

LIKEWISE, THE FACES OF THE DINOSAURS THAT LIVE HERE ARE NEW. WITNESS THE MASTICATORS, A FAMILY THAT, IN THIS ERA OF CHANGE, DOMINATES THE HERBIVORES. A HERD OF THEM IS WALKING PLACIDLY ALONG THE WATER'S EDGE. THEIR HEARING IS KEEN, BUT NONE OF THE PLANT-EATERS SEEMS TO NOTICE A TREMULOUS CRY ARISING FROM THE TANGLE OF ROOTS AT THE EDGE OF THE TROPICAL JUNGLE.

IN THE SAND, COVERED WITH DEAD LEAVES AND SHELTERED BY A DECAYING TREE TRUNK, LIES A NEST.

A CRADLE OF SMALL, SPOTTED EGGS.

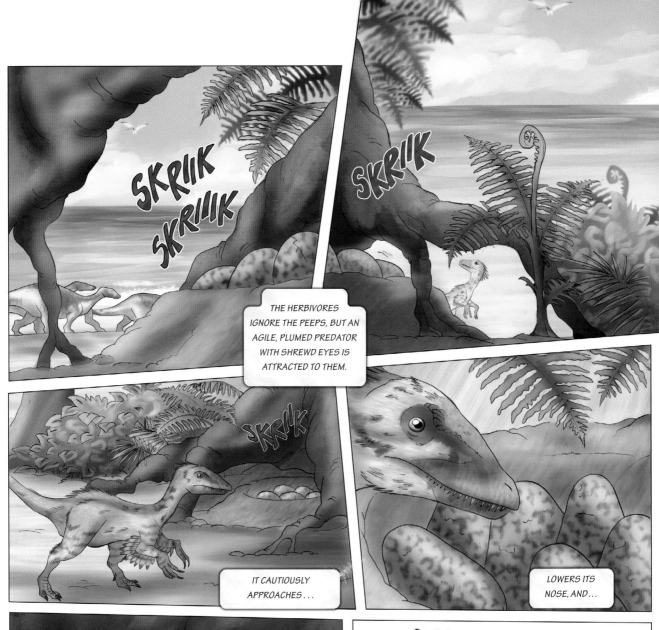

THE HERBIVORES IGNORE THE PEEPS, BUT AN AGILE, PLUMED PREDATOR WITH SHREWD EYES IS ATTRACTED TO THEM.

IT CAUTIOUSLY APPROACHES . . .

LOWERS ITS NOSE, AND . . .

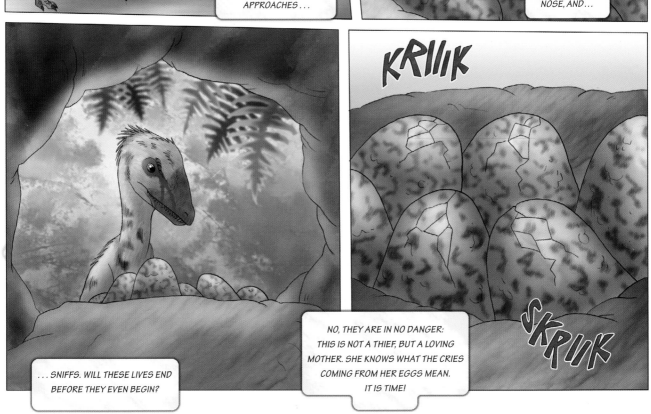

. . . SNIFFS. WILL THESE LIVES END BEFORE THEY EVEN BEGIN?

NO, THEY ARE IN NO DANGER: THIS IS NOT A THIEF, BUT A LOVING MOTHER. SHE KNOWS WHAT THE CRIES COMING FROM HER EGGS MEAN. IT IS TIME!

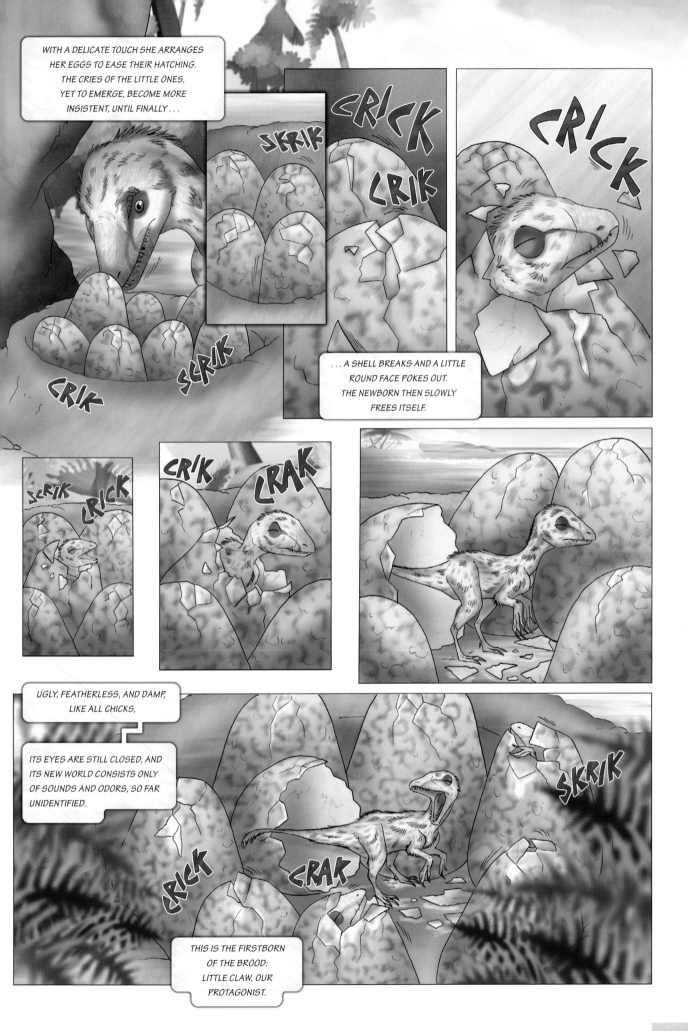

WITH A DELICATE TOUCH SHE ARRANGES HER EGGS TO EASE THEIR HATCHING. THE CRIES OF THE LITTLE ONES, YET TO EMERGE, BECOME MORE INSISTENT, UNTIL FINALLY . . .

. . . A SHELL BREAKS AND A LITTLE ROUND FACE POKES OUT. THE NEWBORN THEN SLOWLY FREES ITSELF.

UGLY, FEATHERLESS, AND DAMP, LIKE ALL CHICKS,

ITS EYES ARE STILL CLOSED, AND ITS NEW WORLD CONSISTS ONLY OF SOUNDS AND ODORS, SO FAR UNIDENTIFIED.

THIS IS THE FIRSTBORN OF THE BROOD: LITTLE CLAW, OUR PROTAGONIST.

A FEW DAYS HAVE PASSED. ALL THE HATCHLINGS ARE FREE OF THE EGGS: IT'S A GOOD YEAR FOR NEW LIFE, THE BROOD HEALTHIER AND MORE NUMEROUS THAN AT OTHER TIMES.

THE MOTHER, THE FIRST THING THEY FOCUS ON AND REECOGNIZE, TRIES TO CALM HER LITTER, BUT IT IS USELESS: EIGHT GREEDY MOUTHS NOISILY DEMAND A MEAL.

EVERY DAY, ALL DAY LONG...

THE CAREFUL MOTHER GUARDS THE NEST, WHILE THE FATHER PROVIDES FOOD.

HERE HE IS, BACK FROM THE FOREST WITH A SIZEABLE LIZARD.

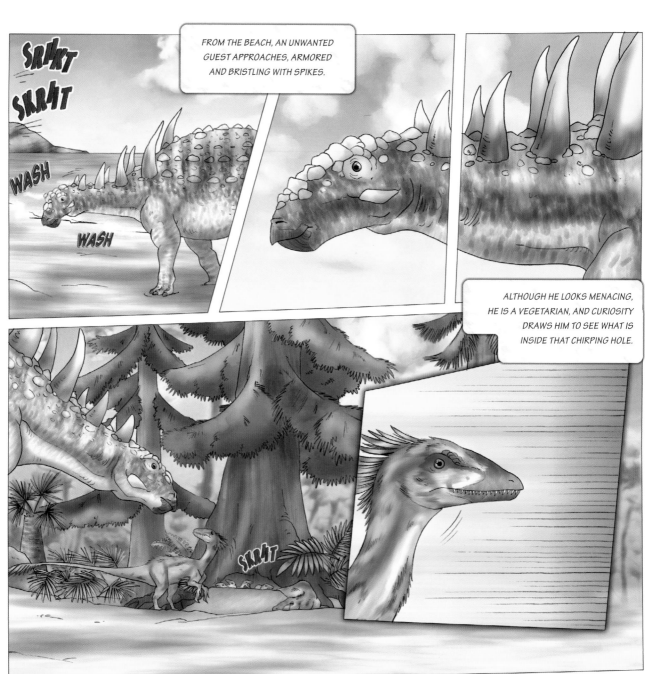

THE FATHER MAKES THINGS CLEAR, AND HURLS HIMSELF TOWARD THE INTRUDER, SNORTING.

THE MOTHER STAYS BEHIND, NEXT TO THE NEST. BRINGING UP THE REAR, SHE KEEPS PUFFING HERSELF UP. SHE HAS HER OWN STRATEGY IN RESERVE, SHOULD THE FATHER FAIL TO SCARE HIM OFF.

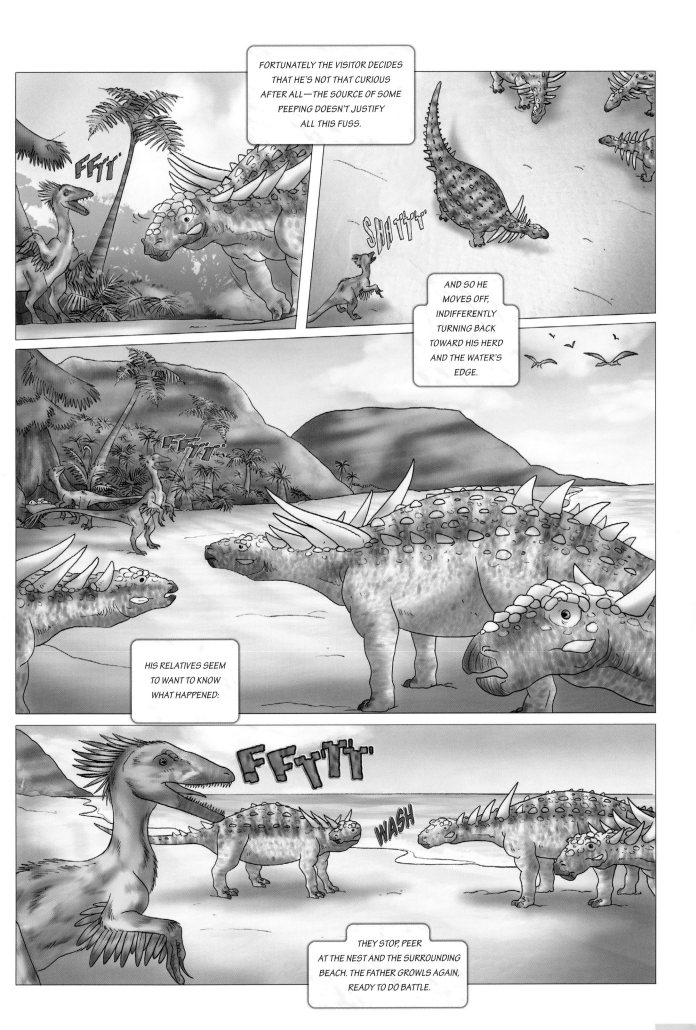

THE MOTHER HURRIES TO COUNT THE CHICKS; FORTUNATELY ALL ARE THERE.

THE HERD OF ARMORED ONES SETS OFF AGAIN, URGED ON BY CONTINUED HOWLS.

WASH

WASH

WASH

SHAKE

SHAKE

IT IS NOT TILL THE STOCKY CREW IS FAR AWAY THAT THE FATHER RETURNS, SHAKING SAND OUT OF HIS FEATHERS.

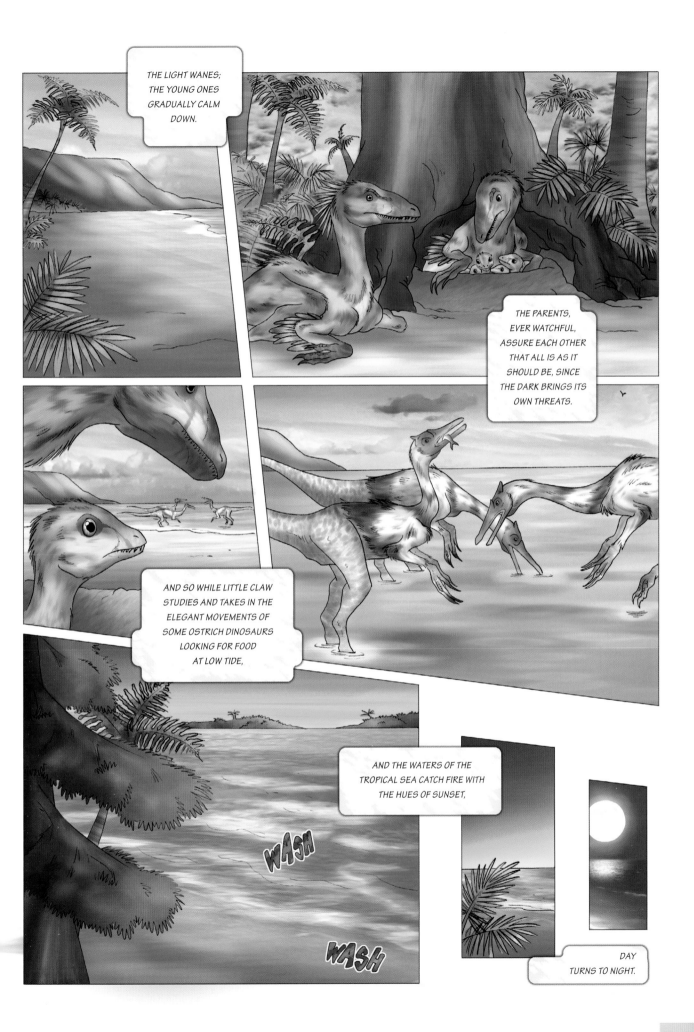

THE LIGHT WANES; THE YOUNG ONES GRADUALLY CALM DOWN.

THE PARENTS, EVER WATCHFUL, ASSURE EACH OTHER THAT ALL IS AS IT SHOULD BE, SINCE THE DARK BRINGS ITS OWN THREATS.

AND SO WHILE LITTLE CLAW STUDIES AND TAKES IN THE ELEGANT MOVEMENTS OF SOME OSTRICH DINOSAURS LOOKING FOR FOOD AT LOW TIDE,

AND THE WATERS OF THE TROPICAL SEA CATCH FIRE WITH THE HUES OF SUNSET,

WASH

WASH

DAY TURNS TO NIGHT.

DAWN. NOT ONE, BUT MANY NIGHTS HAVE COME AND GONE;

A NEW MOON HAS RISEN AND SET SINCE LITTLE CLAW EMERGED FROM HIS EGG ALONG WITH HIS BROTHERS AND SISTERS.

THE CHICKS HAVE GROWN AND ARE NOW SCRAPPY RASCALS WITH SPECKLED PLUMAGE.

GROOVL

EXPLORING THE SHORELINE, THE LARGER WORLD, IS THE ONLY THING THAT LITTLE CLAW AND HIS CREW THINK ABOUT. FROM A TANGLE OF MANGROVE ROOTS, WHERE THEY FEEL SAFE, THREE OF THE YOUNG PREDATORS WATCH THE SLOW ADVANCE OF A TROOP OF LARGE HERBIVORES ALONG THE SHORE.

THE FATHER HAS SHOWN THEM THAT THEIR PREY IS SMALLER.

BUT THE PATIENCE OF THESE NOVICES QUICKLY RUNS OUT; THEIR HUNGER FOR EXPERIENCE IS TOO STRONG, AND SOON A SQUABBLE BREAKS OUT.

OUR LITTLE CLAW IS THE STURDIEST; HE ATTACKS ONE OF HIS BROTHERS, ROLLING IN THE SAND. A SISTER TAKES THE YOUNGER ONE'S SIDE, AND THE TUSSLE BECOMES CONFUSED—

THEN CHAOTIC, AS THE OTHER THREE BROTHERS HURL THEMSELVES INTO THE MIX IN A FREE-FOR-ALL OF KICKS, GRUNTS, AND BITES.

A LITTLE BICKERING IS MAINLY TRAINING THAT STRENGTHENS THE BODIES AND MINDS OF THE IMMATURE PREDATORS.

THE FATHER WATCHES THE FIGHT, LOOKING ON SEVERELY FOR A FEW MOMENTS, THEN MOVES OFF FOR THE HUNT; THE BABIES ARE STILL DEPENDENT ON HIM FOR FOOD.

ONE BROTHER DECIDES TO QUIT, BUT LITTLE CLAW FOLLOWS HIM AND KNOCKS HIM DOWN.

STUMP

THE YOUNG ONE RESPONDS, GROWLING; HE LANDS A BLOW, A BITE.

GROOUL

TRUMP

TUMP

OUR HERO REPLIES IN KIND.

THEY ROLL DOWN OFF A DUNE AND END UP IN A THORNY BUSH, NEAR THE TRANSPARENT WATERS OF THE LAGOON.

STUMP

SFRUSH

SGNAK

THE GAME COMES TO AN ABRUPT END; THE TWO SCAMPS FREEZE WHEN THEIR MOTHER'S WARNING WHISTLE CUTS THROUGH THE MORNING.

FFTTT

NOT FAR OFF, AN ENORMOUS HUNTER WITH LETHAL CLAWS AND A LONG, TOOTHY SNOUT IS INSPECTING THE SHALLOW WATERS IN SEARCH OF HIS LUNCH.

HE IS NOT A USUAL VISITOR HERE; FOND OF FISH, HE IS NONETHELESS ARMED FOR EVERY TYPE OF PREY.

AT HIS APPROACH THE GREATEST CAUTION IS CALLED FOR.

BUT THE LITTLE ONES HAVE SCANT EXPERIENCE; THEY SEE A NAMELESS THREAT AND PRUDENCE IS SWEPT AWAY BY PANIC;

CRAUUR

GROOUUR

THEY FLEE TO THE NEST, DRAWING THE GLOWERING GAZE OF THE LARGE PREDATOR.

HIS FISHING WAS FRUITLESS AND THE MIGHTY RAPTOR IS ANGRY. HE LIKES THE IDEA OF A FAST MEAL.

THUD

THUD

A FEW STRIDES AND THE HUNTER IS NEAR THE NEST.

WITH BRAVERY CLOSE TO CARELESSNESS, SHE TAKES OFF AWAY FROM HER BROOD, CROSSING THE PATH OF THE LARGER CARNIVORE.

HE SLASHES OUT, FIERCELY, SMACKING HIS JAWS, BUT SHE IS ALREADY OUT OF REACH.

SQUISH

SKAK

GROWWR

THE MOTHER'S GAMBLE HAS THE DESIRED EFFECT: HE NOW CHANGES COURSE TO PURSUE HER.

GROUR

THE HUNTER IS BIG AND SWIFT, AND HIS STRIDE IS MUCH LONGER THAN THE MOTHER'S.

FRUSH

FRUSH

HE SEEMS UNSTOPPABLE, BUT HIS STRENGTH AND SIZE ALONE ARE NOT ENOUGH.

SPEED IS THE SPECIALTY OF THE SMALL PLUMED RAPTORS, AND THE MOTHER CONFUSES THE GIANT WITH LIGHTNING-QUICK SWERVES.

THE MOTHER EMERGES FROM HER HIDEOUT, ANXIOUS ABOUT HER YOUNG AND INEXPERIENCED BROOD.

SFRUSH

FITTT FITT

AT THE NEST, THE FATHER RALLIES HIS CHILDREN WITH GURGLING SOUNDS.

LITTLE CLAW IS SCOLDED WITH WARNING BITES; IN THE FUTURE HE WILL HAVE TO BE MORE CAREFUL.

THE DANGER AVERTED TODAY WILL CLEARLY NOT BE THE LAST.

A HARD, DANGEROUS LIFE LIES AHEAD FOR THE YOUNG ONES.

TWICE, THE MONSOONS HAVE COME AND GONE.

THE LONG-NOSED PREDATOR IS IDENTIFIABLE NOW; HIS ATTACK IS STILL A VIVID MEMORY FOR LITTLE CLAW, WHO IS NO LONGER A BABY.

AS AN ADULT, HE RESEMBLES HIS FATHER AND LIVES ALONE.

SPLASSSSH

WASH

WASH

ALL HIS SIBLINGS HAVE ALSO GROWN AND MATURED; SOME HAVE DECIDED TO FORM A SMALL CLAN WITH THEIR PARENTS, WHILE OTHERS HAVE LEFT FOR NEW SHORES, LIKE OUR HERO.

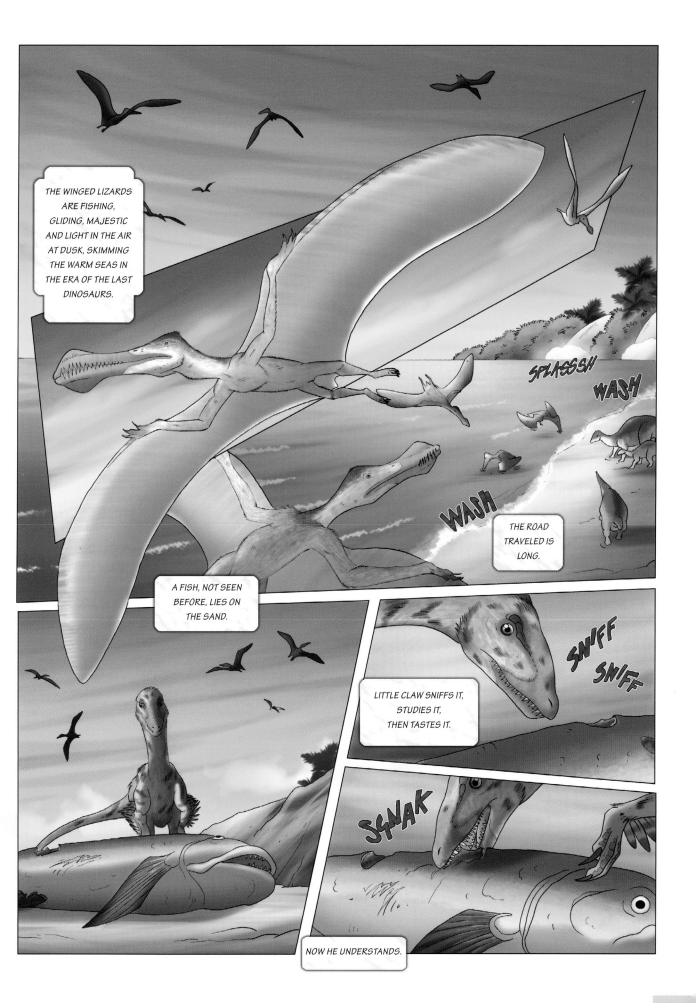

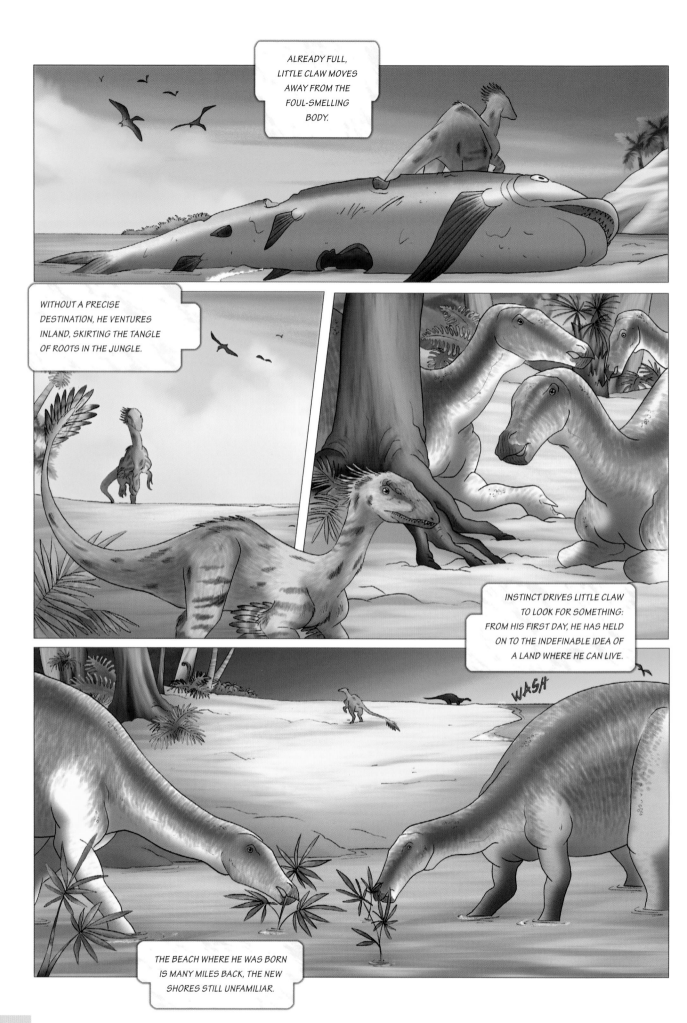

ALREADY FULL, LITTLE CLAW MOVES AWAY FROM THE FOUL-SMELLING BODY.

WITHOUT A PRECISE DESTINATION, HE VENTURES INLAND, SKIRTING THE TANGLE OF ROOTS IN THE JUNGLE.

INSTINCT DRIVES LITTLE CLAW TO LOOK FOR SOMETHING: FROM HIS FIRST DAY, HE HAS HELD ON TO THE INDEFINABLE IDEA OF A LAND WHERE HE CAN LIVE.

WASH

THE BEACH WHERE HE WAS BORN IS MANY MILES BACK, THE NEW SHORES STILL UNFAMILIAR.

THE NEST WAS HIS WORLD, AND HOWEVER LARGE HE THOUGHT IT WAS, WHAT REMAINS TO BE EXPLORED AND KNOWN IS SO MUCH LARGER.

WASH

WASH

WASH

BEFORE HE COULD SEE, LIFE WAS ALL NAMELESS SOUNDS AND ODORS, AND HIS YOUTH WAS SPENT LEARNING THEIR DIFFERENCES, MAKING SENSE OF IT ALL, TO PREPARE FOR LIFE AS AN ADULT.

WASH

WASH

HE NOW KNOWS ABOUT SO MANY THINGS, BUT SO MUCH MORE AWAITS HIM AHEAD.

DINOSAUR EVOLUTION

This diagram of the evolution of the dinosaurs (in which the red lines represent evolutionary branches for which there is fossil evidence) shows the two principal groups (the saurischians and ornithischians) and their evolutionary path through time dur-ing the Mesozoic. Among the saurischians (to the right), we can see the evolution of the sauropodomorphs, who were all herbivores and were the largest animals ever to walk the earth. Farther to the right, still among the saurischians, we find the theropods. Among the theropods there quite soon emerges a line characterized by rigid tails (Tetanurae), from which, through the maniraptors, birds (Aves) evolve. The ornithischians (to the left), which were all herbivores, have an equally complicated evolutionary history, which begins with the basic Pisanosaurus type but soon splits into Thyreophora ("shield bearers," such as ankylosaurs and stegosaurs) on the one hand, and Genasauria ("lizards with cheeks") on the other. The latter in turn evolve into two principal lines: the marginocephalians, which include ceratopsians, and euornithopods, which include the most flourishing herbivores of the Mesozoic, the hadrosaurs.

IDENTIKIT *(see page 6)*

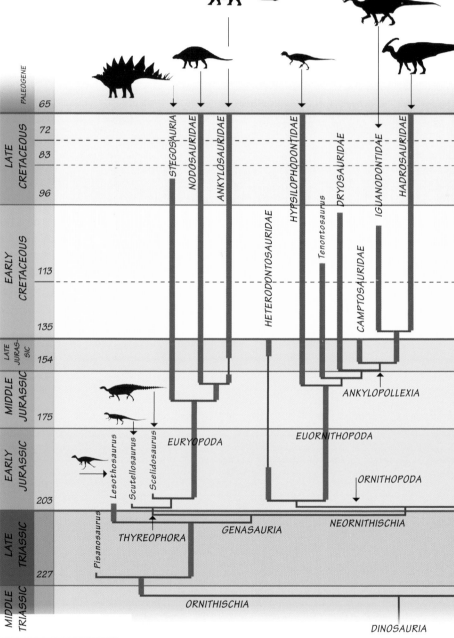

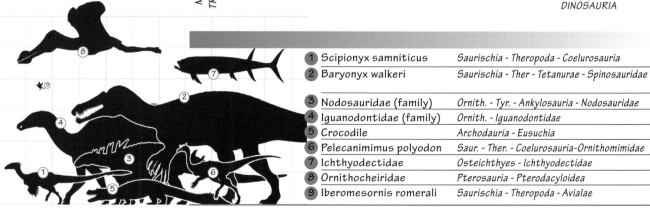

1	Scipionyx samniticus	*Saurischia - Theropoda - Coelurosauria*
2	Baryonyx walkeri	*Saurischia - Ther - Tetanurae - Spinosauridae*
3	Nodosauridae (family)	*Ornith. - Tyr. - Ankylosauria - Nodosauridae*
4	Iguanodontidae (family)	*Ornith. - Iguanodontidae*
5	Crocodile	*Archodauria - Eusuchia*
6	Pelecanimimus polyodon	*Saur. - Ther. - Coelurosauria-Ornithomimidae*
7	Ichthyodectidae	*Osteichthyes - Ichthyodectidae*
8	Ornithocheiridae	*Pterosauria - Pterodacyloidea*
9	Iberomesornis romerali	*Saurischia - Theropoda - Avialae*

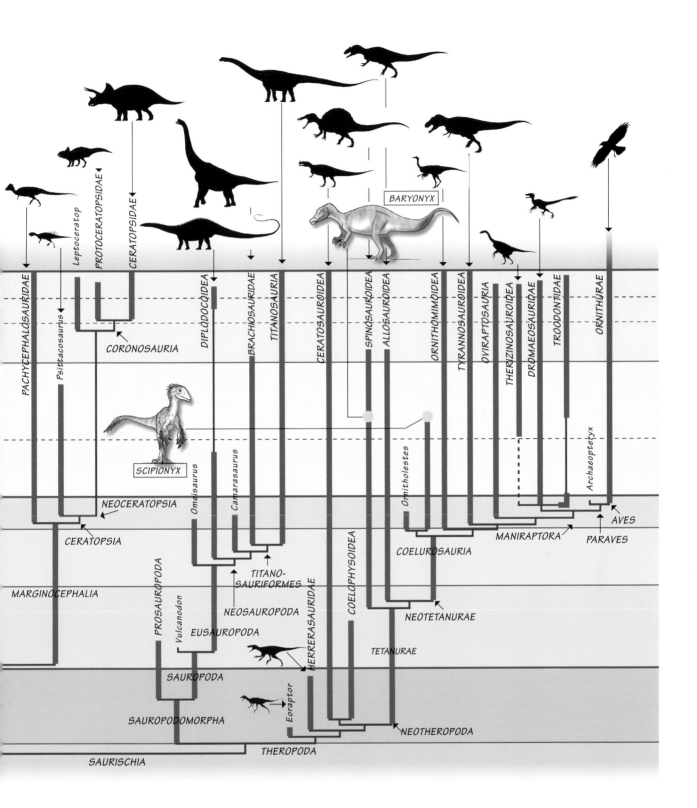

LENGTH	HEIGHT	WEIGHT	DIET	PERIOD	TERRITORY
over 6 feet	20 inches at the shoulders	110 lbs.	meat	Early Cretaceous (Aptian-Albian)	Italy
over 28 feet	6½ feet at the shoulders	over 6,600 lbs.	meat, fish	Early Cretaceous (Aptian-Albian)	England, Spain, North Africa
over 13 feet	over 3 feet at the shoulders	over 3,300 lbs.	plants	Early Cretaceous (Aptian-Albian)	Europe
over 16 feet	5 feet at the shoulders	over 4,400 lbs.	plants	Early Cretaceous (Barremian-Albian)	worldwide
over 6½ feet		up to 110 lbs.	fish	Early Cretaceous (Aptian-Albian)	Italy
5 feet	20 inches at the shoulders	up to 110 lbs.	omnivorous	Early Cretaceous (Barremian-Albian)	Spain
up to 6½ feet		over 66 lbs.	meat, other fish	Early Cretaceous (Aptian-Albian)	Tethys Ocean
wingspan: over 19 feet	unknown		fish	Early Cretaceous (Aptian-Albian)	worldwide
wingspan: approx. 6 inches	unknown		insects	Early Cretaceous (Barremian-Albian)	Spain

41

THE CRETACEOUS

BIRTH, LIFE, AND DEATH

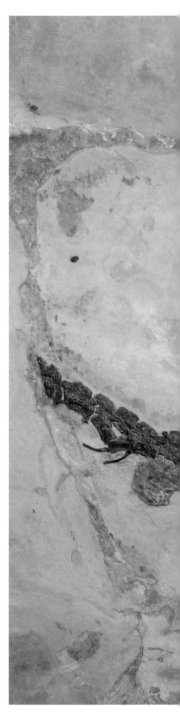

Pietraroja

The Cretaceous was a period of change: a time of triumph and fall, glory and pain for the dinosaur kingdom. However, this period began without incredible geological or climatological upheavals, leading some scholars to think that a biological crisis might have marked the end of the Jurassic.

Flora and fauna did not change much between the Late Jurassic and Early Cretaceous; what did change during the Cretaceous was the number of epicontinental seas. In fact, it seems that during the final period of the dinosaurs, the sea engulfed many areas that are now above sea level. Consequently, paleontologists have discovered fossil remains that were increasingly well-preserved throughout this era and help cast light on a world whose splendors we can only imagine.

One of these fossil sites is a small outcropping on a mountain in Campania: the Pietraroja deposit. Unknown to most people, it hides

✳1
page 16
panel 3

◀ Illegal excavations in the Pietraroja deposit in the Matese Mountains of Campania. Note the stratified gray limestone that makes up the deposit.

priceless treasures for a paleontologist. One of the most important—yet one of the least studied—dinosaurs in the history of paleontology comes from this very place. This is *Scipionyx* ✱1, the protagonist of our story: a meat-eating dinosaur, only a single specimen of which has ever been found. Even this specimen is a very young animal, a dinosaur that perhaps had only recently emerged from its egg.

The story of *Scipionyx*, which might intrigue the best mystery writers, will probably never be fully clear. What we do know is that since 1998, two Italian scholars—including one of the authors of this book—have been presenting the facts we have to the world, creating quite a stir in the process.

▲ *Scipionyx samniticus. The skeleton of this theropod baby was prepared with great care, although it still has not been fully studied. Note the head, which is large compared to the body; the large eye sockets; and the short nose: these are all signs of the animal's young age at its death. It is also possible to see internal organs, particularly the intestines and certain muscle areas, beneath the tail and above the front limbs. Some vertebrae are separated from their neural spine, another sign of the specimen's youth.*

What makes *Scipionyx* so important in the dinosaur world? Not its size: the fossil measures little more than eight inches, minus a tail. Yet while it may have been a small carnivore, "Skippy," as it has been nicknamed in English, provides an answer to many questions and, as always happens in paleontology, raises many new ones.

Let's begin with prehistoric Italy. Until around the late 1980s, experts thought that Italy had simply been a seabed during the Mesozoic era; certainly land animals would not have been able to live there, and consequently the most common answer to the question, "Were there dinosaurs in Italy?" was a flat "No." Then researchers discovered an increasing number of tracks, such as those at Lavini di Marco or those near Bari (now destroyed), which told us that dinosaurs— large ones—did wander the Italian peninsula. And so the image of a prehistoric Italy completely submerged in the waters of the Tethys Ocean gave way to that of one composed of islands and archipelagos.

Then the first flesh-and-blood "Italian" dinosaur arrived: *Scipionyx*. The expression "flesh-and-blood" is not inappropriate for this amazing theropod, because the fossil is not just a pile of bones: it also contains preserved soft tissue. Therefore, in addition to providing tangible proof that dinosaurs did, indeed, exist in Italy, *Scipionyx* was also the first dinosaur fossil to be discovered with some of its internal anatomy partially intact.

Today, thanks to discoveries in the Jehol **biota** in China, we have grown almost accustomed to

dinosaur specimens containing muscles, internal organs, and perfectly preserved feathers. But in 1998 a dinosaur fossil that seemed like a sort of X-ray was something entirely new. And for the paleontological community, that is precisely what *Scipionyx* represented: a snapshot of a dinosaur with many of its internal organs preserved, and in a position that it presumably assumed while alive.

Finally, the fossil was that of a theropod baby. Specimens of young plant-eating dinosaurs were already available to science at the close of the twentieth century, but young theropod specimens, particularly ones with such an abundance of detail, were a novelty. In short, *Scipionyx* had everything it took to become a star.

The principal reason for its well-deserved fame, however, can be found in the Pietraroja deposit itself. In the second book in this series we became familiar with the discipline of taphonomy, and we saw how, in specific deposits, it is possible for internal organs and soft tissue to be preserved and to fossilize. In fact, you may recall the jellyfish fossils and the *Archaeopteryx* feathers from the Solnhofen deposit. From this standpoint the Pietraroja deposit is very similar to more famous sites, such as those in southern Bavaria or in the Jehol biota in China. We have already described the processes that led to the formation of such exceptional fossils, but Pietraroja had a unique environment. It was not characterized by a coastal lagoon, as in Germany, or a series of continental lakes subject to **periodic volcanism**, as in China. And it is surprising that the first

▲ *An example of a perfectly preserved Coelodus, a shellfish-eating fish. Note that remains of these fish are abundant at Pietraroja, but their prey is practically absent, a sign that these fish did not live there.*

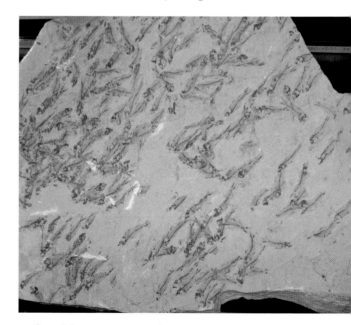

▲ *One of the most common discoveries at Pietraroja consists of these tiny fish, Clupavus, fossils of which are often found in very numerous groups.*

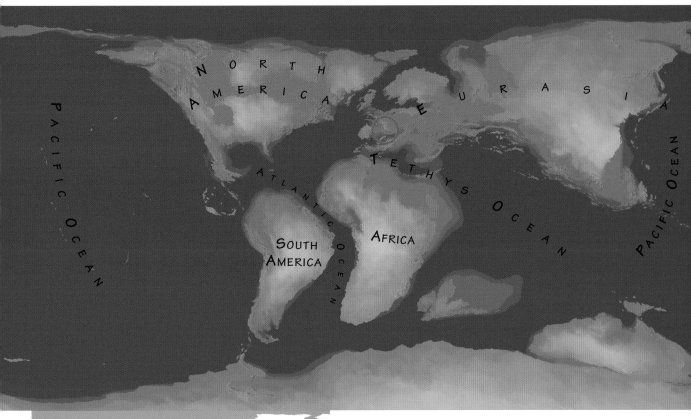

▲ *The probable appearance of the Earth during the Early Cretaceous. The red circle shows the location of Pietraroja, in an archipelago in the Tethys Ocean.*

▶ *Stratigraphic division of the Early Cretaceous. It is interesting to note that various deposits similar to Pietraroja are concentrated in a period that stretches from the Albian to the Aptian, although their origins and environments are different from one another. Our story unfolds during the Albian.*

CRETACEOUS	UPPER CRETACEOUS	Maastrichtian	72–65 mya
		Campanian	83–72 mya
		Santonian	87–83 mya
		Coniacian	88–87 (85?) mya
		Turonian	92–88 mya
		Cenomanian	96–92 mya
		Albian	108–96 mya
	LOWER OR EARLY CRETACEOUS	Aptian	113–108 mya
		Barremian	117–113 mya
		Hauterivian	123–117 mya
		Valanginian	131–123 mya
		Berriasian	135–131 mya

serious studies of this deposit did not take place until 2005, since people had known about Pietraroja and its marvelous fossils since 1798.

In fact, the earliest fossil fish from this deposit were curiosities in the courts of Europe, and according to some scholars, the kingdom of Naples offered them as gifts, in some cases to other European powers. However, an extensive scientific investigation of Pietraroja was never considered, although limited attempts were undertaken, and many other factors contributed to the lack of in-depth information about the site. In any case, Pietraroja was long thought to be a coastal lagoon, but in 2005 a series of analyses yielded no evidence of such a lagoon, instead lending support to a different interpretation: that during the Cretaceous, Pietraroja was a sort of underwater collection pit. In fact, during the

Early Cretaceous, the region where fossils of fish and other animals are now found lay at the end of a long underwater channel or system of channels into which sand, sediment, and carcasses flowed. These occasionally also included land animals, such as our *Scipionyx*. In this broad, shallow pit, sediment was deposited and bodies were rapidly covered over, thereby producing the specific type of fossilization we discussed in our second book.

This exceptional fossilization has allowed scholars to discover numerous interesting specimens: fish that lived off shellfish, complete skeletons of which have been discovered with their delicate mouths perfectly preserved; early crocodiles, which probably lived near the water; lizards that hunted insects on dry land; small invertebrates, including starfish and shrimp,

spectacularly preserved; large predator fish, such as the beached ichthyodectoid in our story ✳2; and, of course, the incredible *Scipionyx*.

Again, the fossil of this small dinosaur is preserved to an exceptional degree. Delicate structures such as the trachea, along with all the creature's bones, arranged as they were in life—scholars call this "life position"—are visible down to the smallest details. Various areas of the body have retained their soft tissue: chest muscles, tail muscles, and the entire intestine. A reddish blotch at the center of the chest area might even be the animal's liver, a possibility about which there has been much speculation but no conclusive agreement among scientists.

We know that this *Scipionyx* is a baby because of details such as the large eye socket and the nose, which is noticeably short in comparison to the rest of the skull, but also because neither the forefeet nor the vertebrae are fully **ossified**. Some vertebrae (which are composed of separate bony elements) are not completely fused together. And on the claws of the front limbs, the keratin covering—like that of our fingernails—is perfectly preserved.

What can we learn from *Scipionyx*? First of all, we can see how a dinosaur is "built" on the inside. We know the position of the various organs, at least the digestive organs. For example, thanks to this small specimen we now know that dinosaurs' (or at least theropods') intestines did not rest

▲ *One of two crocodile specimens discovered at Pietraroja, still being studied by an Italian-Spanish team. Note the perfect preservation— and the missing part of the pelvis, the result of an error during excavation.*

▶ *A photo of Scipionyx under ultraviolet light, revealing the soft tissue areas as yellowish against the blue background and the brown of the bones. The light blue areas are the glue applied to consolidate the fossil.*

✳2
page 37
panel 3

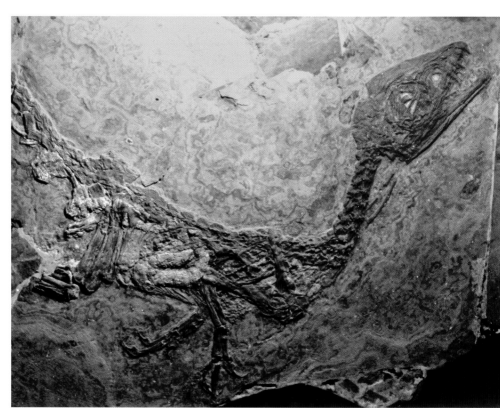

upon their pubic bones, as was hypothesized in the past. Unfortunately, poor handling during the collection of this small fossil has deprived us of certain interesting details, such as the hind limbs, the tail, and probably—a still greater loss—the animal's coat of feathers.

Kinship relationships between *Scipionyx* and other dinosaurs have not yet been completely mapped out, but for the moment this carnivore tends to be grouped among the relatives of dromeosaurs. In technical terms, *Scipionyx* is a representative of the same **basal group** from which animals such as the famous *Velociraptor* would later be derived. The common ancestor of *Scipionyx* and dromeosaurs lived before both of them and started at least two evolutionary lines, one of which developed further into dromeosaurs while the other, which included *Scipionyx*, retained its primitive characteristics, resulting in animals that, during the dinosaur era, could be considered living fossils.

Probably the primitive characteristics of Scipione Claw—this is, in fact what *Scipionyx* means—also derive from this small carnivore's having lived in areas isolated from the rest of the world. **Insular fauna** often have very distinctive characteristics. For example, another dinosaur discovered in Italy, a hadrosaur that has yet to be given a scientific name, has attributes, such as a different hand structure, that make it very different from all other hadrosaurs. Dwarf hadrosaurs have been discovered in Romania, and until a few thousand years ago, elephants the size of large dogs lived in Sicily. Islands often contain hidden biological surprises, and they sometimes allow the survival of living fossils. Think, for example, of Australia, with all its marsupials; or of Komodo, inhabited by the largest living lizard, the famous Komodo dragon; or of New Zealand, home to the tuatara, a rare reptile similar to a large lizard. It is possible, then, to imagine *Scipionyx*'s territory as an island, an archipelago, or a region isolated in some other way from the larger world of the Cretaceous. Unfortunately, until Pietraroja and its star dinosaur are studied further, we will not have more in-depth information on this subject.

▼ *An enlargement of the area with soft tissues in the Scipionyx fossil. From left to right, it is possible to see a muscular mass at the base of the tail; the large intestines, where it is even possible to discern the folds; a reddish area around the elbows, which has been interpreted as the remains of the liver; and another muscular mass, beneath the neck, which has not been specifically identified, and within which the remains of the trachea can be glimpsed.*

The Dinosaurs of the Early Cretaceous in Europe

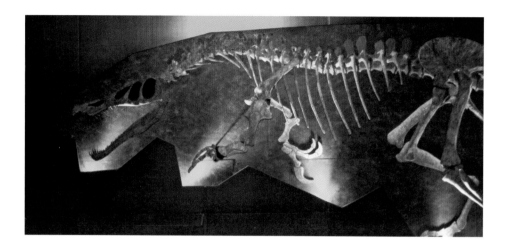

◀ Baryonyx walkeri *mounted in the dinosaur section of the Natural History Museum in London. Note the crocodile-like snout and the large claws on the front limb, from which the animal gets its name.*

▼ Pelecanimimus. *This was the first ornithomimosaur discovered in Spain; portions of its soft tissue, including even red blood cells, are perfectly preserved. The environment in which this animal fossilized was a continental lake.*

In our story we also encounter other dinosaurs. Of these, the largest and most dangerous to the protagonist is an animal first discovered in England, called *Baryonyx* **✱3**.

This name means "heavy claw," or "large claw," and in fact this animal's principal characteristic is the enormous claw on each of its hands. Its skeleton is that of a typical biped predator, with a head somewhat like a crocodile's. Because fish scales were discovered inside the fossil, it has been hypothesized that *Baryonyx* used its claws the way modern bears do, for fishing. There is a complex debate surrounding this animal, however. On the one hand, scientists have discovered that the "Surrey Claw," as this dinosaur is known in England, is related to one of history's largest and most dangerous carnivores: *Spinosaurus*. On the other hand, recent studies conducted in England have demonstrated that the skull of *Baryonyx* worked like that of certain crocodiles, such as the gharial, which specialize in feeding on fish. If we base a hypothesis solely on the movements of the skull, we might conclude that *Baryonyx* fed exclusively on fish; yet the structure and dimensions of the animal would seem to fit a predator of land animals as well. It is for posterity to judge, as they say.

In addition to this dangerous carnivore there were other theropods of moderate size, including certain species of allosaur and some very peculiar dinosaurs, such as *Pelecanimimus* **✱4**. This is a primitive ornithomimosaur, or ostrich dinosaur, discovered in Spain, also in a zone of special fossilization. Along with bones, sections of the skin and muscles of this strange animal have been discovered. This might seem like something out of the science fiction of *Jurassic Park*, but don't worry (or be disappointed, as the case may be!): we are still a long way from obtaining dinosaur DNA. Even if we could obtain it, science is not yet technically capable of cloning entire extinct animals from DNA alone. *Pelecanimimus*, however, is interesting because its fossil provided the first chance for scientists to closely examine an ornithomimosaur beak, an organ that has always

✱3
page 29
panel 2

✱4
page 25
panel 4

▲ Spinosaurus aegyptiacus. *The cranium and teeth of this carnivorous dinosaur were adapted to a diet that surely included both herbivorous dinosaurs and fish. Perhaps* Spinosaurus *and* Baryonyx *are really examples of the same genus; in that case,* Spinosaurus *would have lived in a territory that ranged from Africa to England.*

✱5
page 15
panel 1

✱6
page 20
panel 1

been mysterious. In fact, we have learned that this "pelican mimic," which is the meaning of the Spanish dinosaur's name, had a hornlike beak that covered its jawbones and was equipped with small teeth, much like the beaks of ducks. If you've ever seen a duck sift its food from the water, you will have some idea of how *Pelecanimimus* may have eaten. This discovery is especially valuable considering that even today, scientists are uncertain about what ornithomimosaurs' diet contained.

Among herbivores, *Iguanodon* is probably the most famous dinosaur of the Early Cretaceous, and it was the second dinosaur to be described after *Megalosaurus*. All dinosaur enthusiasts know the story of the "iguana teeth." A doctor from the English countryside, Gideon Mantell, discovered some of this animal's teeth, which none of the experts of the time were able to identify correctly. Then Mantell himself noted their similarity to the teeth of present-day iguanas. In the newspapers, Mantell tried to credit the discovery to his wife, who in an ironic twist left him years later because of his excessive passion for fossils.

Remains of *Iguanodon*, one of the most widespread dinosaurs known, can be found practically everywhere, even in Australia. This animal, like *Camptosaurus* in our last book, had sets of teeth—still primitive compared to what we will see in hadrosaurs—and was a facultative biped;

that is, it could walk on either two or four legs. It probably lived in groups; the complete remains of thirty-nine individual animals were found in Bernissart, Belgium alone, though paleontologists still do not agree about the genesis of this deposit. In our story, however, we encounter a relative of *Iguanodon*, which was more "advanced" from an evolutionary standpoint ✱5, and which we hypothesize descended from *Ouranosaurus*.

The Early Cretaceous also saw the further development of armored dinosaurs, and in our story we meet *Polacanthus* ✱6, a primitive ankylosaur from the Nodosauridae family whose skull is known to scientists only in fragmentary remains. While still primitive, this quadruped ornithischian exhibits many of the characteristics that made its descendants famous: heavy dermal armor, enormous defensive spikes (indeed, its name means "many-spiked"), a stocky body, and a sturdy tail.

For many paleontologists, dinosaurs represent much more than dead bones with labels to be debated. These were very active animals, and we will try to understand how they lived and how they behaved—at least to the degree that we can hypothesize on a scientific basis. Our story continues, but we must await its next installment before we can examine the dinosaurs of the Cretaceous in greater detail.

The Biology of Dinosaurs

▶ *Scipionyx in pursuit of a primitive mammal. Note the coat of feathers of at least two types (long feathers on the front legs and tail, down on the body), which, as far as we know, is a distinguishing characteristic of all small and average-size theropods. A great deal of the information regarding this aspect of dinosaur biology comes from the spectacular discoveries in the Jehol biota in China.*

Biology is a word that originally meant "discourse on life," but today it has taken on a profoundly different meaning. Present-day biologists engage in chemical and genetic analyses in laboratories, almost always forgetting that the organisms whose chemistry and genetics they are studying were originally alive and part of a complex ecosystem. With a nod to its original meaning, however, we will use the term biology to indicate our study of the *life* of dinosaurs. We are going to discover how these dominant creatures lived, how they ate, how they attacked and defended themselves, how they reproduced, and also how they died.

Like all organisms on earth, dinosaurs were "living machines"; that is, they were governed by a series of well-defined metabolic processes. All dinosaurs had to breathe, eat, drink, expel waste, reproduce, and defend themselves from danger. We know very little about dinosaur metabolism—that is, the whole of the organism's chemical and physical functions. This is because metabolism does not fossilize, nor, in most cases, do an animal's internal organs. However, we can make educated guesses about many dinosaur

characteristics from the fossils that we do have at our disposal.

First of all, there is the age-old question of warm-blooded versus cold-blooded. Dinosaurs were once considered reptiles—and many people still consider them to be so—but as far as scientists can tell, they were as different from modern reptiles as we are. Moreover, in modern zoology the idea of "warm-blooded" or "cold-blooded" is disappearing, as we have seen that regulating body temperature is not solely typical of mammals and can be influenced by many factors. It would be more correct to speak of *poikilothermia*, the inability to regulate one's body temperature, and *homeothermia*, the ability to regulate it. (Let's try to remember these two terms, at least until the end of this book!) We are used to thinking that animals such as lizards or fish are poikilothermic, but some readers will be surprised to learn that many sharks, tuna, and swordfish are, for all practical purposes, homeothermic.

But let's get back to dinosaurs. We will never know with certainty whether they were homeothermic or poikilothermic, but we have already seen, in the third book of this series, that sauropods were probably *gigantothermic*; that is, they maintained a constant body temperature thanks to their enormous mass. And other dinosaurs? We know that advanced theropods, at least small ones, were plumed. According to many scholars, having feathers automatically indicates homeothermia, but these scholars tend to forget that feathers and quills may have originally appeared for many other purposes, for example as a means of communication. It is clear that quills insulate a body, and thus we can reasonably suppose that small theropods were homeotherms. But what about large carnivores, such as *Allosaurus* or *Tyrannosaurus*? We take for granted that these animals, by extension, were also homeotherms, yet we are almost certain that they were not covered with feathers. Some say that they were covered with down, or that the young at least were plumed. In fact, this is still a thorny question. Defenders of the idea of homeothermic theropods point to the structure of these animals ("built to be active") and their kinship with birds as proof. Their opponents note that some bone structures seem to rule out homeothermia. The problem arises only in some cases, because Mesozoic climates were for the most part hot and constant. But how did *Allosaurus* manage to hunt during the Australian winter, for example? We can hypothesize that "polar" dinosaurs evolved behaviors that protected them from the cold—for example, migrations toward warmer areas—but we cannot be certain.

What about ornithischians? They were all rather large animals, with the exception of some basal groups. Is it possible that they, too, were in some way homeotherms? Yes, but once again we will probably never know for sure, barring the invention of a time machine.

Metabolism leads us to another subject of fierce debate among paleontologists. How did dinosaurs breathe? Here the paleontological world is divided into three camps. There are those who look to birds, the specialized descendants of a group of theropods, as the answer to all biological questions concerning dinosaurs, and maintain that all dinosaurs breathed with air sacs, like birds (in which these sacs form a kind of outpocketing of the lungs). This hypothesis is supported by such dinosaur characteristics as trabeculae or "hollow" bones, uncinate processes (small protuberances on the ribs of some theropods), and other birdlike features; these, however, could also be explained in other ways. The second camp takes the opposite side and maintains that since no evidence exists linking dinosaurs' breathing with birds', we must assume that dinosaurs breathed with lungs alone.

The problem is complicated, because not only is direct observation impossible, we are also dealing with two schools of thought that almost take on the rigidity of dogma. The true case, as supported by a third camp, probably lies somewhere in between. We know that some dinosaurs had air sacs, because birds have highly developed ones, and it is possible that in small theropods air sacs were used as a "supplementary breathing system" during brief, rapid sprints. However, air sacs are not sufficient for breathing on dry land for animals weighing more than 330–440 pounds; moreover, some animals that breathe with lungs—elephants, for example—have hollow bones without also having air sacs. (The hollow bones make their skeletons lighter and more elastic despite their size and weight.)

We can conclude, then, that as a general rule dinosaurs had a respiratory system based on lungs, but that small theropods, at least, may have been able to use air sacs as a respiratory aid—that is, whenever they needed to be "turbocharged."

The discovery of *Scipionyx* has opened up a new series of discussions regarding the internal anatomy of dinosaurs. Before the discovery of this little animal, the internal anatomy of a dinosaur was entirely a matter of speculation. For example, paleontologists thought that the enlargement of the **dista**l portion of the pubis— the "pubic boot"—in theropods was an adaptation to support their intestines, as well as an attachment point for their muscles. We now know that their intestines did not reach all the way to the pubic boot, just as we now know that dinosaurs were equipped with a trachea made up of cartilaginous rings—although we are still unsure if the rings were open, like those in mammals, or closed, like those in birds. We also know that the livers of baby dinosaurs were quite large. This can mean many things, but it is not an unknown phenomenon in birds, for example. According to some scholars, it might indicate that dinosaurs used a "hepatic pump"—in other words, that their livers acted as a pump to assist breathing, similar to what occurs in crocodiles. This interpretation has, however, aroused consid-erable opposition, mainly due to the uniqueness and immaturity of the specimen on which studies have been based. It is true that our *Scipionyx* is a very young individual, as well as the only member of its species to have been recovered thus far. This means that any study of it must take into account both the possibility of anatomical change during growth—which is extremely normal in **tetrapods**—and the possibility of its being a specimen with malformations. This is not a very frequent occurrence, but it has happened before in paleontology.

In compensation, we do know that this small dinosaur's intestines must have had an excellent capacity for absorption, given the large number of folds with which they seem to be covered. This should not be surprising, since the absorption of food is fundamental for an animal that is still growing. Unfortunately, the discovery of dinosaurs with preserved internal organs is unusual, and despite some exceptional finds in the Jehol biota in China, and in other complete

hadrosaur "mummies," our understanding of the internal anatomy of dinosaurs is still quite vague.

The same holds true for dinosaurs' muscles. One of the first things one learns in texts about dinosaurs is that scholars can reconstruct the arrangement of their muscles based on studying what are known as muscle scars, namely, the marks left on bones by the muscles that were attached to them. This notion is completely theoretical, however; not all muscles are directly attached to bones, and it is not always possible to know everything about a given muscle just by examining muscle scars. Consequently, the reconstruction of dinosaurs' muscular apparatus is by no means complete or certain. We will look at one important result of this uncertainty when we discuss movement and predatory behavior.

To conclude this brief look at the internal anatomy of dinosaurs, we should point out that sometimes scientists are not even sure about the arrangement of their bones! Remember that fossilization is a rare event and that the dinosaur skeletons we discover are almost always very incomplete. When only some of a dinosaur's bones have been found, therefore, paleontologists base their reconstruction on a characteristic typical of most animals, especially tetrapods: symmetry. We know that if we imagine a plane that cuts an organism in half lengthwise—the

sagittal plane, technically speaking—the two resulting parts will usually be mirror images of each other. This characteristic can sound banal and obvious, but it is precisely what allows one to proceed to the reconstruction of dinosaurs. Moreover, in general there are few skeletal differences within an animal group, and so not only obvious characteristics—two arms and two legs, a tail, and a neck—but also subtler ones will carry across the group; for example, the front limbs of tetrapods are generally made up of a finite number of bones, which are identical from species to species (although it is important to remember that there are always exceptions).

This knowledge is useful when one is working on related animals. For example, if we have the complete skeleton of *Allosaurus*, we know that any other allosaurid that is discovered should be constructed like *Allosaurus*, and so experts literally model the missing bones—in resin, plaster, or some other material—on the basis of the known bones of another, related type. This is why we always see complete skeletons in museums.

Unfortunately, the process is never as simple as it sounds. For example, even today we do not know how the plates of stegosaurs were arranged. And we should remember, as we learned in book three of this series, that no actual *Apatosaurus* cranium was found until the 1980s, so for nearly

one hundred years reconstructors of this sauropod placed the head of a *Camarasaurus* on its neck. It can also happen that we will find only a very small portion of an animal. This is the case with the famous *Deinocheirus*, of which the only remains we have are exactly two arms. We still do not know to what family of animals they belong—there are various hypotheses that lie outside the scope of this book—but generally we associate them with either Ornithomimidae or another, similar family (though a minority of paleontologists believe that the bones belong to a **therizinosaur**).

But dinosaurs, as we have said, are more than fossil remains. Millions of years ago they were alive, and thus had behaviors for attacking, defending, **foraging**, courting, and so on. How, then, do we go about studying dinosaurbehavior? We can make educated guesses about some behavioral patterns—mainly those related to attack and defense, as we will see—but others are extremely complicated, and for many we will never have a definitive understanding. But let's see what we can do to bring these animals, which so dominated our planet in the Mesozoic, back to life.

First of all, by studying the fossil remains of dinosaurs it is possible to try to understand the use of certain specific parts: teeth, claws,

◀ *A reconstruction of* Baryonyx, *starting from the known bones. First the missing portions of the skeleton and then the muscles are reconstructed, the latter based principally on the muscular structure of birds and crocodiles, but also on muscular scars, that is, marks showing where the muscles were attached to the bones.*

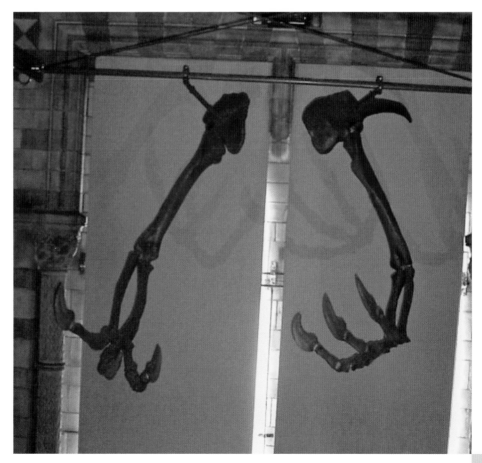

▶ Deinocheirus mirificus, *a theropod discovered in Mongolia and about which little is known. The only portion of this animal that has been recovered is the front limbs, and paleontologists still disagree about this enormous animal's classification and biology.*

defensive structures. Based on these, we can hypothesize about the dinosaurs' principal behaviors for attack and defense.

Let's start with attack. Predators are built like killing machines; their entire skeletons reflect this function. Thus, the first thing we can learn from predators is their "weapon of choice." For example, in large carnivores the lower portion of the body—rear limbs and tail—seems structured to propel the animal forward, while the true weapon is the mouth, bristling with long, powerful, serrated teeth set into strong, narrow jaws, capable of inflicting extremely serious wounds or cutting small prey in half. The bite of these large carnivores does not seem to resemble that of modern big cats, which tend to suffocate their prey or break their necks. On the contrary, large theropods seem to have skipped the "niceties" and functioned almost like moving guillotines. Thus the primary weapon of *Allosaurus*, *Tyrannosaurus*, and similar enormous predators was their powerful bite.

But what about smaller dinosaurs? Their front limbs are longer, and they are equipped with sharper and thinner claws, capable of inflicting considerable wounds. Yet if we look at the teeth

of small theropods, we see that these, too, are structured to do the greatest harm, and so it is possible that their primary weapon was the same. When *Deinonychus*, the first dinosaur with a sickle-shaped claw, was discovered in the late 1960s, paleontologist John Ostrom hypothesized that this animal and others like it used the two large claws on their hind limbs to rip open the belly of their victims. But current detailed analyses have shown that these claws had practically no cutting capacity, while the coordinated use of the front limbs—which in some ways recall those of a mantis—and the powerful bite made even small predators dangerous for every herbivore. This lack of variety in hunting weapons should not be surprising. After all, if we reflect on the history of human warfare, we also see that the best and most effective weapons are only variations on the same principle: a weapon capable of piercing the adversary, penetrating the body, and striking the vital organs. It is no accident that Macedonian

▼ *A praying mantis. Structurally the front legs of small theropods are very like those of a mantis, and many of their movements were probably similar to the predatory movements of this exceptional insect. Such gestures might have been the origin of flapping flight.*

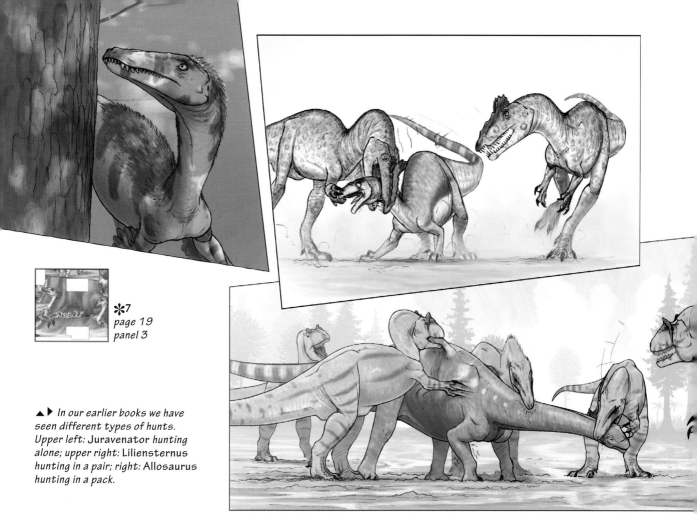

❋7
page 19
panel 3

▲▶ In our earlier books we have
seen different types of hunts.
Upper left: Juravenator hunting
alone; upper right: Liliensternus
hunting in a pair; right: Allosaurus
hunting in a pack.

phalanxes, Roman legions, and Renaissance-era pike squads all had a type of spear as their main weapon. And so the main weapon for the dominators of the Mesozoic remained the bite—a powerful, devastating, and very rapid bite, driven by a sinuous and muscular neck, just like that of birds.

But were these bites inflicted by lone hunters or by a number of animals at the same time? Most fossilized tracks that appear to have been left by theropods engaged in hunting are the tracks of solitary specimens. Paleontologists have discovered what may be evidence of at least one hunting pack: a deposit of various Deinonychus specimens fossilized together with a single Tenontosaurus specimen. This find has always been presented as clear evidence that Deinonychus hunted in a pack, and also that its preferred prey was this unfortunate ornithopod. Yet a hunting expedition yielding a single prey but also leading to the loss of at least five of the hunters is not a good long-term proposition for a pack. Moreover, all studies done on this exceptional find barely take into account the possibility of a taphonomic artifact (do you remember this term from previous volumes?).

Did carnivorous dinosaurs, then, live alone or in packs? This, too, is a question that will probably never be answered, and in fact, in our stories we have seen both systems of hunting. It is possible that small theropods—for example, Liliensternus, in our first book, or Scipionyx ❋7, in this one—lived in family groups or hunting groups, and we might hypothesize the same about large theropods based on indications of violent struggles among members of the same species. Certainly the pack itself would have been another weapon, bringing with it the possibility of taking down prey much larger than an individual hunter could fell—as with the Allosaurus pack in our third book. Unfortunately, we will have to be satisfied with indirect evidence, and with keeping all options open. For now we say that theropods may have hunted in packs, at least some of the time. The work of the paleontologist is full of uncertainty!

In contrast, the abundance of defensive systems found in prey is surprising. The first and most obvious defensive weapon is speed. Essentially, if you want to avoid being struck, you have to be able to move away from the spot where your adversary's blow will land. An attack always has a high level of inertia, because it must be quick, and consequently a predator cannot change the direction of attack at the last moment in order to "correct its aim." Many modern animals have markings that serve as false targets to protect their vital regions from attack; certain coral reef fish, for example, have false eyes on their tails. We may never know whether any dinosaurs had coloration that employed this false target technique, but we can conjecture that some small ornithischians were structured for rapid sprints.

We are not in a position to know how fast herbivores or carnivores were able to run; no matter how many studies have been published, the truth remains that it is nearly impossible to be sure about any values proposed. Not only are we missing data for calculating the speed of an animal that is extinct and without direct descendants, but we often tend to forget that in nature, animals very rarely run—they do it only when necessary—and so we really need to calculate sprinting speeds rather than running speeds. What is the difference? Running is a sustained action; there are very few tetrapod runners: **canines** among mammals, **ratites** (flightless birds) among birds, and human athletes, who train specifically at this activity for years. Sprinting, however, is a rapid and almost instantaneous action; the cheetah, often cited as the fastest extant animal, is capable of reaching very high levels of speed, but only for a few seconds, after which it must stop. Thus the problem is determining not how rapidly our dinosaurs ran, but rather how rapidly they sprinted. We can hypothesize that sprinting was a component of predators' attacks, but also a useful defensive weapon for potential prey.

Not all herbivorous dinosaurs, however, functioned this way, and indeed it appears that sprinters were a very small minority. The evolutionary trend, in most **phyletic lines** of herbivores, was toward an increase in size. And so we will see how other defensive systems evolved in order to contend with theropods' increasingly powerful weapons.

Being large in and of itself is an extremely valuable defensive system. Try to imagine having to eat a pizza 40 feet high and nearly 80 feet across. Things would get even more complicated if the pizza in question had the habit of moving in order to squash you. This is probably how defense worked for gigantic sauropods. They were far larger than any of their possible predators, and they may have been able, if the need arose, to rear up on their hind limbs for a few moments—just enough time to bring their front limbs down on

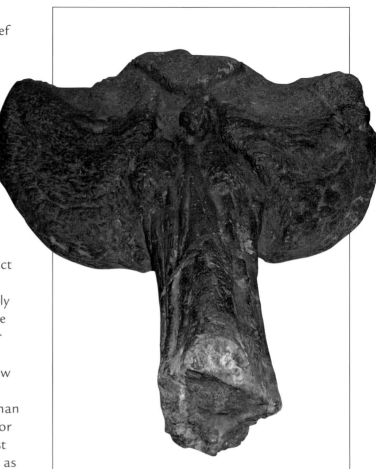

an unfortunate predator. We can only imagine the damage that such an attack might have inflicted.

According to some experts, sauropods' tails could also be used for defense. A Canadian scholar has hypothesized that some sauropods used their tails almost like whips to smack their enemies. We know that the crack of a whip is caused by its tip traveling faster than the sound in a sort of miniature sonic boom, and so the hypothesis is that *Diplodocus* was able to crack its tail similarly. Incredibly, this model might in fact work—but once again, we will never know with certainty.

Another form of defense that large size allows is the "convoy." We know from various tracks we have discovered that sauropods moved in herds, and that they probably kept their young at the center of the group. Thus they formed a convoy in which both numbers and, above all, size provided a passive defense. For a predator it would have been like attacking a moving fortress while armed only with a steak knife. We humans also use

◀ *The tails of ankylosaurs were equipped with veritable "ironclad clubs," like those of ancient and medieval warriors. A blow inflicted by this sort of weapon could easily incapacitate any predator.*

the convoy system when we have to protect transports, as in the Battle of the Atlantic during World War II, for example. Forming convoys has an added benefit: it makes choosing a target difficult for the predator, as we saw in our third book. In the modern-day African plains these herds are often made up of different species; the same strategy would have been completely reasonable for dinosaurs.

And yet there were herbivorous dinosaurs that were not overly concerned about safety in numbers, preferring another strategy entirely. Armed predators? These potential prey armed themselves as well.

The first implementers of this defensive system were the ornithischians of the Thyreophora, a name that, not coincidentally, means "shield bearers." Stegosaurs had dermic shields, as we saw in our third book, although it is unlikely that these functioned defensively. However, in their close relatives, ankylosaurs, these bony shields were fused together, one against another, to form a complete coat of armor, sometimes more than four inches thick ✳8. It would practically have taken an antitank missile to break through, and theropods were not equipped with these!

◀ *The "wall of shields" of ceratopsids, used against a predator. A defense of this kind may have turned this group of herbivores into an impenetrable fortress, with sharp bony points turned both upward and forward—a predator's two possible directions of attack. The raised collar also made the animal seem taller than it actually was. Appearing larger or taller, or even showing bright colors, often dissuades even the hungriest predator from completing its attack. This type of defense is by no means rare in nature.*

✳8
page 23
panel 3

✳9
page 22
panel 2

Moreover, on the back and sides of this armor, many ankylosaurs had enormous, bony spines, just in case of an emergency ✽9. But thyreophores embodied the saying "You can't be too careful," and so in addition to defensive dermal armor, they also evolved an offensive arsenal. The tail of nearly all thyreophores was a lethal weapon. Stegosaurs were "satisfied" with four bony spikes about three feet long at the end of their tails, while ankylosaurs wielded a veritable club, bony and iron-hard, as we will see in detail in our sixth book. The resulting weapon was similar to those used by medieval infantry to pierce the superior armor of wealthy knights: clubs, hammers, and morning stars (spiked clubs). Thus a predator attacking a thyreophore would have found itself in enormous trouble; in fact, many paleontologists

▼ Pentaceratops *at the Oklahoma Museum of Natural History in Norman. This is the ceratopsid with the largest cranium in relation to its body length.*

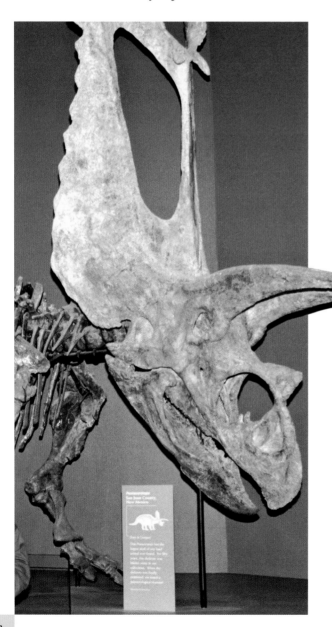

believe that some adult thyreophores did not have natural enemies.

Ceratopsids, too, could rely on force, but they were not armored like knights. They had long, massive horns on their heads, which, when the head was held in a normal position, usually pointed upward, but when the animal lowered its head, pointed forward. But there is more: if we look at a ceratopsid cranium, we see that these animals were equipped with a large, bony collar. If the animal lowered its head, the collar also moved into a vertical position. This approach mirrors the "wall of shields" defense used by the Vikings, in which soldiers' multicolored shields formed a solid barrier while their spears thrust out to deter attackers. In the same way, the collars of ceratopsids, perhaps also colored, might have inspired fear (while being too delicate to act as truly effective shields). Moreover, many of these animals were very tall; from the dimensions of the collars of chasmosaurs, such as *Pentaceratops* on this page, whose collar covers half its body, we can imagine how tall they would have been when upright. The collars often sported spines and points that were turned backward when the head was in a normal position but became deterrents when the collar was held vertically, as when a predator attempted to go around the "wall."

Faced with all these lethal defensive weapons, predators must have had wretched lives—or at least we might expect as much. But without successful predators, prey grow in an uncontrolled fashion and then die out as they consume all the resources. We know from fossil evidence that this didn't happen, and that in fact predators flourished. So what was their secret? To begin with, not all of the prey animals' defenses were impenetrable. A mistaken movement by a stegosaur might have condemned it to a clash with numerous aggressors. An isolated ceratopsid would have been able to stand up to one predator, but not to two or three attacking from different directions. In addition to overwhelming the prey with greater numbers, there is another, equally valid method of hunting: attacking individuals that are young, old, or ill. This is precisely what goes on in modern ecosystems, and it is possible that predators waited for such an animal to become isolated from the others, either through fatigue or inexperience (remember *The Journey*?), so that dinner would be assured. The young are the most vulnerable members of a species, and realizing this leads us to an investigation of another

◀ A Psittacosaurus nest discovered in Liaoning, China. Notice the empty space in the center, where the parent may have stayed to sit on the eggs, and the nearly complete skeletons of the babies, buried and perhaps killed by a volcanic eruption.

▼ The mating of two plateosaurs. We still know relatively little about dinosaur reproduction, but it is very likely that their reproductive organs were more like those of crocodiles than those of birds.

aspect of dinosaurs' daily life: reproduction.

How did dinosaurs reproduce? There is no precise data on the subject, of course, but here, too, we can come up with some fairly good hypotheses. Let's begin with the final product of reproduction: the egg. We know that dinosaurs were **oviparous**; that is, they laid eggs from which their young were born. Dinosaur eggs were not laid at random, and scholars have established that different dinosaur species had different ways of placing them. For example, as we will see in our next story, some sauropods laid eggs in a line, while ornithopods laid them in a circular arrangement and may have nested in large colonies. We hypothesize that certain carnivores nested near herbivore colonies so that they could capture the young of inattentive parents and feed their own broods. That both carnivorous and herbivorous dinosaurs displayed parental care ✳10 is also posited by many scholars. One thing we do not know, however, is what the reproductive apparatus of dinosaurs was like. We can gain an idea from the pathologies—that is, malformations—discovered in some fossil eggs; if we had to base our assumptions on that data, we might venture a hypothesis that dinosaurs' reproductive systems more closely resembled those of crocodiles than those of birds. All things considered, this is not very strange; remember that while birds are a type of dinosaur, they are very specialized and adapted to a specific environment, the air.

✳10
page 18
panel 7

✳11
page 17
panel 1

✳12
page 31
panel 4

Let's return briefly to the subject of parental care, however. Many scholars now believe that dinosaurs watched over and protected their young in some fashion. This behavior is typical of animals that lay a smaller number of eggs ✳11; they must act in such a way that a sufficient number of young reach adulthood. The best method of accomplishing this is usually to stay near the babies, protecting, feeding, and raising them. Like modern big cats, carnivorous dinosaurs may have behaved in this manner, teaching their young to hunt and watching out for external dangers ✳12. For example, some *Triceratops* remains show the marks of teeth of an adult *Tyrannosaurus* and of at least one baby, and some scholars offer the explanation that a mother *Tyrannosaurus* brought this food to her young. Other paleontologists maintain that various markings discovered in hadrosaur nests indicate parental care on the part of herbivores as well.

Indeed, the name of the North American hadrosaur *Maiasaura* implies precisely such parental care (*Maiasaura* means "good mother reptile"). The problem is that not all specialists agree on how to read the very few traces that have survived from the past, and so there is no consensus about how dinosaurs cared for their young; at this point, however, all scholars accept the idea that they were at least reasonably caring parents.

Finally, malformations and pathologies, or the traces left by diseases and injuries, constitute another interesting body of evidence, and there is a branch of paleontology, called paleopathology, that is concerned specifically with the study of this evidence. Essentially, all damage to the skeleton, whether from attacks by other animals, illnesses, or accidents, is examined and catalogued. In this way it is possible to piece together a sort of clinical picture or medical history—albeit a very limited one—of dinosaurs. And in this way we know that dinosaurs suffered fractures, bone malformations, tumors, and other illnesses that leave traces on the skeleton. Paleopathology also allows us to draw additional conclusions about dinosaur behavior, predation, and even parental care. For example, those adult and baby *Tyrannosaurus* teeth marks on the same animal may indicate that the mother tyrannosaur brought prey to her young. *Tyrannosaurus* bite wounds on the head of another *Tyrannosaurus* tell us of fights between these enormous predators, perhaps over territory or a kill. And that not all attacks by predators were successful—as is also the case today—we know thanks to the discovery of bite lesions that show signs of advanced healing, a clear indication that the attacked animal managed to escape and regain its health.

All in all, dinosaur behavior is an extremely fascinating field of study. And although it forms the basis for the paleontological study of these animals, modern science too often pushes it into the background in favor of routine and eternal debates about how similar dinosaurs are to their descendants, birds. But it is precisely the study of paleobiology—that is, the biology of animals from the past—that allows us to see dinosaurs not as bones to be labeled and catalogued, but as living, powerful animals, the supreme rulers of a past era. In our next book ✳13 we will see the beginning of the end of that era, when the largest animals ever to appear on earth roamed the lands that now make up Argentina. After they vanished, creatures of that size would never exist again.

▲ *Maiasaura guarding her nest. This hadrosaur provided the first evidence of parental care in dinosaurs, as its name, meaning "good mother reptile," indicates.*

✳13
Volume 5
Giant versus Giant:
Argentinosaurus and
Giganotosaurus

GLOSSARY

Basal group: in cladistics (the classification of organisms based on the branchings of descendant lineages from a common ancestor), a set that contains the ancestors of a phyletic line.

Biota: the totality of life forms, both animal and plant, that characterize a certain region or geographic area.

Canines: the family of carnivores (mammals) that includes dogs and wolves.

Distal: situated farthest away from a point of reference.

Foraging: searching for and gathering food.

Insular fauna: animals that live on islands, whether physical islands in the sea or other environments isolated from the rest of the world by physical barriers (such as impassable mountains), and that usually exhibit features distinct from similar animals inhabiting more diverse ecosystems.

Ossified: formed of bone; here referring to the aging process through which skeletal parts originally made of cartilage in the young turn to bone and become more resistant and rigid over time.

Oviparous: laying eggs as a means of reproduction.

Periodic volcanism: the repetitive occurrence of eruptions of magma at more or less regular periods.

Phyletic line: a theoretical family lineage whose members have direct ancestor-descendant relationships, that is, are directly tied to one another in an evolutionary chain without branchings.

Ratites: the group of flightless birds that includes ostriches.

Tetrapods: vertebrates with four limbs; that is, all vertebrates from amphibians onward.

Therizinosaur: a member of a group of theropods characterized by very long, three-toed front limbs with blade-like claws; a lack of teeth; and rather prominent abdomens. Paleontologists still disagree about much of the biology of this group, including its diet.

Acknowledgments

For their help and support both direct and indirect, Matteo Bacchin would like to thank (in no particular order) Marco Signore; Luis V. Rey; Eric Buffetaut; Silvio Renesto; Sante Bagnoli; Joshua Volpara; his dear friends Mac, Stefano, Michea, Pierre, and Santino; and everybody at Jurassic Park Italia. But above all he thanks his mother, his father, and Greta for the unconditional love, support, and feedback that have allowed him to realize this dream.

Marco Signore would like to thank his parents, his family, Marilena, Enrico di Torino, Sara, his Chosen Ones (Claudio, Rino, and Vincenzo), la Compagnia della Rosa e della Spada, Luis V. Rey, and everybody who has believed in him.

DINOSAURS

1 THE JOURNEY: *Plateosaurus*

We follow the path of a great herd of *Plateosaurus* from the sea—populated by ichthyosaurs—through the desert and mountains, to their nesting places. Their trek takes place beneath skies plied by the pterosaur *Eudimorphodon*, and under the watchful eye of the predator *Liliensternus*.

We discover what life was like on our planet during the Triassic period, and how the dinosaurs evolved.

(In bookstores now)

2 A JURASSIC MYSTERY: *Archaeopteryx*

What killed the colorfully plumed *Archaeopteryx*? Against the backdrop of a great tropical storm, we search for the perpetrator among the animals that populate a Jurassic lagoon, such as the small carnivore *Juravenator*, the pterosaur *Pterodactylus*, crocodiles, and prehistoric fish.

We discover how dinosaurs spread throughout the world in the Jurassic period and learned to fly, and how a paleontologist interprets fossils.

(In bookstores now)

3 THE HUNTING PACK: *Allosaurus*

We see how life unfolds in a herd of *Allosaurus* led by an enormous and ancient male, as they hunt *Camarasaurus* and the armored *Stegosaurus* in groups, look after their young, and struggle amongst themselves. A young and powerful *Allosaurus* forces its way into the old leader's harem. How will the confrontation end?

We discover one of the most spectacular ecosystems in the history of the Earth: the Morrison Formation in North America.

(In bookstores now)